W9-AVX-575

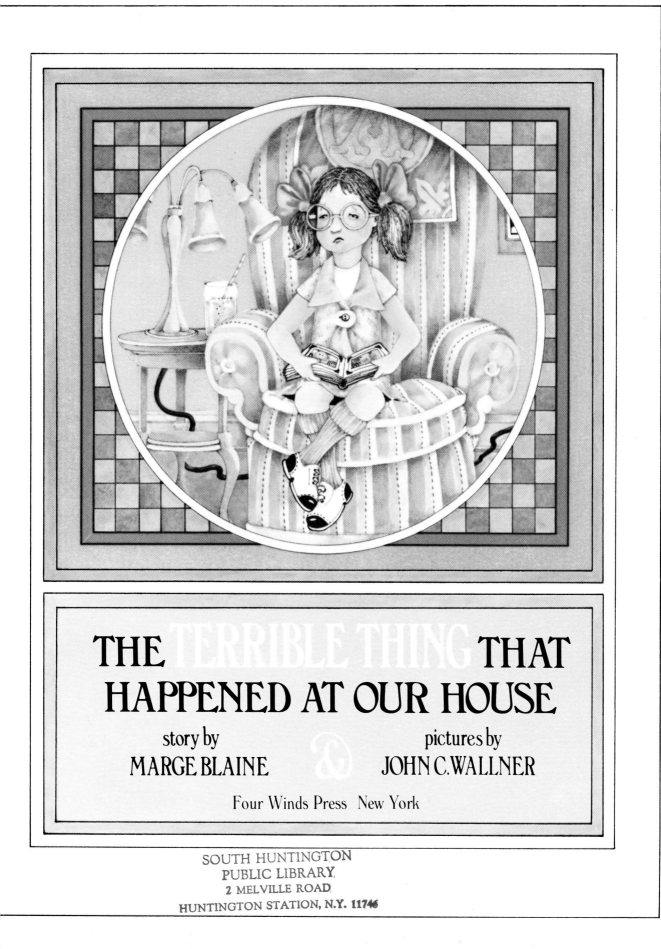

THE TERRIBLE THING THAT HAPPENED AT OUR HOUSE

story by
MARGE BLAINE

&

pictures by
JOHN C. WALLNER

Four Winds Press New York

Text copyright © 1975 by Marge Blaine
Illustrations copyright © 1975 by John C. Wallner

Four Winds Press
Macmillan Publishing Company
866 Third Avenue, New York, NY 10022
Collier Macmillan Canada, Inc.

Printed in the United States of America

10 9 8 7 6 5

Library of Congress Cataloging-in-Publication Data

Blaine, Marge.
    The terrible thing that happened at our house.

    Summary: A youngster relates the terrible problems that
occurred after her mother went to work and how the family
solved them.
    [1. Mothers—Employment—Fiction. 2. Family life—
Fiction] I. Wallner, John C., ill. II. Title.
[PZ7.B5372Te   [E]   86-4827
    ISBN 0-02-710720-5

To my mother, who has always been a real mother

My mother used to be a real mother.

In the mornings, when my brother and I left
for school, she'd kiss us and wave goodbye.
"Have a nice day, darling. Be good, honey,"
she'd say as we went out the door.

When we came home for lunch, we'd have toasted cheese sandwiches or tuna on a bun. Then chocolate pudding or a cupcake for dessert—with sprinkles.

After school she'd listen to us tell about who got
punched in the stomach, or what happened to Abby
on the stairs, or how the teacher yelled when I
dropped my box of colored markers all over the floor.
Then she'd pour us a glass of milk and give us a snack.

Afterwards we'd go outside or have friends come and play at our house. My mother always had time to read to us and help us make things and take us to the park.

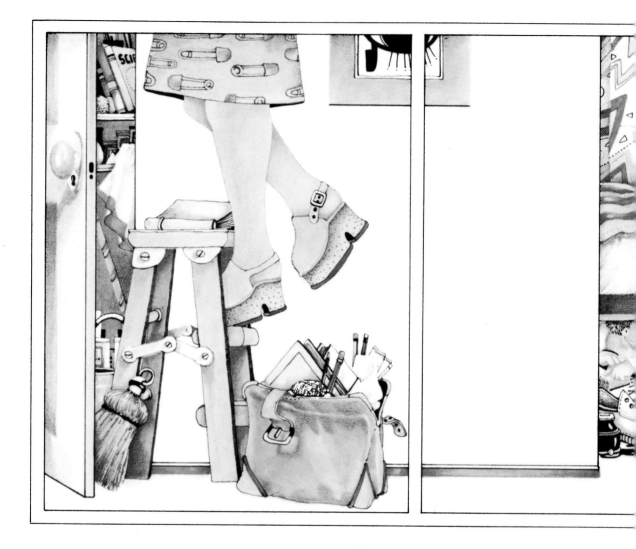

My mother went back to being a science teacher.
She said it was important work.
I always thought taking care of us was pretty
important, but she said we could do a lot more for
ourselves than we did.

That's when everything began to be different.
In the mornings we had to rush around making
our own beds and clearing the table because my
mother was busy getting ready to leave, too.
We even had to find our own underwear and socks.

We had to eat lunch in school because there was
no one home at lunchtime anymore.

I HATE EATING LUNCH IN SCHOOL.

The lunchroom smells like fish or frankfurters...

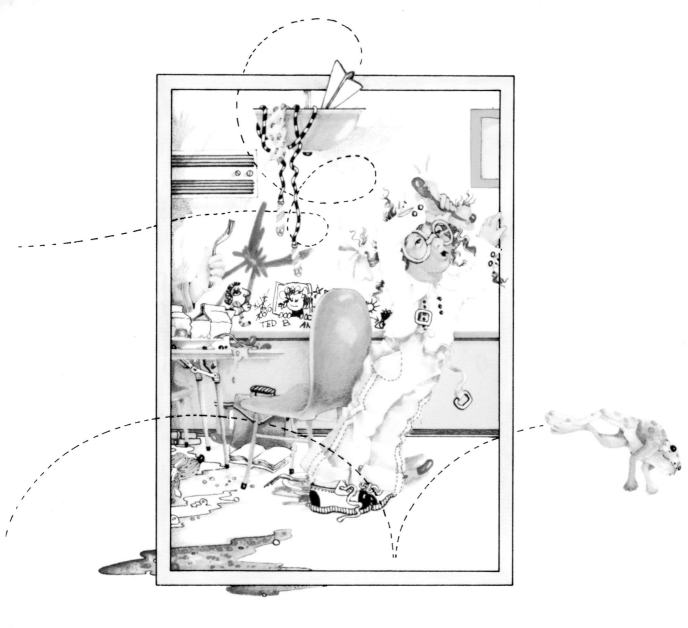

And all that yelling gave me a headache.

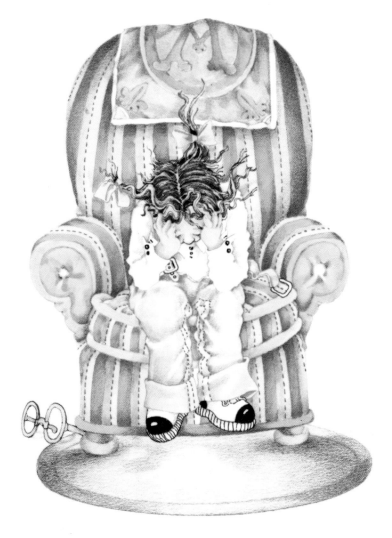

After school, instead of listening to us the way she
used to, my mother would say, "I need a few minutes to
clear my head, kids—I've had a really tough day."
And once, when I told her how the teacher kept me in
at recess just because I sharpened my pencil three times
during math, she said, "You must have been annoying
her, dear," instead of being on my side.

My father used to be a real father, too. He'd come home from work and say, "Hi, everybody—what's for dinner?" Then he'd listen to my brother and me talk while he washed up and changed. He told us things about his office or about what happened on the way to work. When we finished eating dinner, he'd clear the table while my brother and I did our homework or watched TV. And later, maybe he'd have time for a game.

My father used to read us stories every night before we went to bed. And on Saturdays he always took us to the garage with him, and we'd watch while he got gas for the car and had the oil changed or the spark plugs cleaned.

But that's all different now, too.

My father began coming home with packages from the
supermarket. "I'll get dinner tonight," he'd say.
And then he'd tell us we were having frozen salmon
croquettes or meatballs in wine sauce.

I HATE SALMON CROQUETTES AND MEATBALLS IN WINE SAUCE.

They smell like what we have for lunch in school.

Yichhhhhh!

My brother and I had to clear the table after dinner
while my father did the dishes with my mother.
Sometimes he did them all by himself while she marked
tests or planned tomorrow's lesson in the living room.
And half the time he didn't read us stories,
because he was too busy helping to fold laundry.

I tried reading to my brother, but he picked
boring books and asked dumb questions.
My mother had the car serviced at a place near her
school, so we never got to go to the gas station
with my father anymore.

My parents said we were all much happier now.

Then, one night at dinner, when my brother kept
talking and talking, and no one was really listening
to him or even heard me when I asked for some more
milk, I got mad. I got so mad I started yelling.

ANYMORE IN THIS HOUSE.

NO ONE HELPS YOU.

PASSES THE MILK

NEED IT!"

Everyone stopped talking and looked at me.

My mother said, "Oh, you poor thing," and came
and put her arms around me.
My father said, "What's bothering you, sweetheart?"
And my brother passed me the milk.
I told them how I couldn't stand all this rushing
around every morning. And how I hated eating lunch
in school. And how no one had time to hear what
happened to me during the day. And how I was sick
and tired of missing stories and talks and games
and everything.

My parents really listened this time and then they
said, "Let's see what we can do."

They decided that if we all got up a little bit earlier,
and my father left for work a little bit later, we
could get out in the morning without so much rushing.
My mother asked Louisa, who lives next door, if we
could eat lunch at home with her kids. She said,

"Sure," except on Fridays when she goes for her
allergy shots. And Ellen, our babysitter, began
to come for an hour after school. Now my mother
has a little time to herself for clearing her head
or reading the mail or doing a wash. Some afternoons
we help to dust, or just pick up. Then she feels
more like making things with us, or walking to the park.

My brother and I said we could fold the laundry
so my father would have time to read us a story.
The socks don't always come out right, but
we're getting better.
We take turns choosing what to have for supper.
Sometimes I go to the supermarket with my father,
and my mother is teaching my brother and me
how to make hamburgers. The plain kind.

And after we clean up in the kitchen and get our work done, most nights there's still time to play a game. Or talk together.

Things aren't so terrible at our house anymore.
I guess they're a real mother and father after all.